"Currier is adept at drawing a fine line between the erotic and the tragic, and at telling stories that 'although personal, are also the stories of our community.'"
—The New York Times Book Review

"A writer who consistently surprises and delights, Currier's dynamism will surely carry his literary career to higher heights."
—Bay Area Reporter

"The breadth of Currier's personal experience is evident in his writing, which is moving without resorting to melodrama, familiar without feeling clichéd."
—Windy City Times

"As a writer, Currier should be lauded for his creative decision to avoid the all-too-common formulaic trappings of most current novels written for and about gay men."
—Lambda Literary

Also by Jameson Currier

A Gathering Storm

Based on a True Story

Dancing on the Moon: Short Stories about AIDS

Desire, Lust, Passion, Sex

Mr. Darcy's Pride

Paul's Cat

Still Dancing: New and Selected Stories

The Devil's Cake

The Forever Marathon

The Haunted Heart and Other Tales

The Third Buddha

The Wolf at the Door

Until My Heart Stops

What Comes Around

Where the Rainbow Ends

Why Didn't Someone Warn You About Prince Charming?

THE CANDLELIGHT GHOST

AN ILLUSTRATED TALE BY

JAMESON CURRIER

Chelsea Station Editions

New York

The Candlelight Ghost
Story and Illustrations by Jameson Currier

Book design by Peachboy Distillery & Designs
Published by Chelsea Station Editions
www.chelseastationeditions.com
info@chelseastationeditions.com

Print ISBN: 978-1-937627-85-0
Library of Congress Control Number: 2023931185

First Edition

The Candlelight Ghost

CANDLELIGHT THEATER
SOLD

When Otto Meloso, a fifty-year-old accountant, bought the Candlelight Theater in Candler, everyone told him he was doing a very foolish thing, as there was no doubt that the place was a money pit and he, of all people, should know this intuitively because of his history with financial investments. In fact, Sybil Carroway-Green, whose family had owned the theater for decades and who had managed the last seasons of the theater before it went dark, felt it her duty to mention the fact to Mr. Meloso when they met to negotiate the property.

"After the last fire, I brought in all sorts of consultants to bring the building up to code," Mrs. Carroway-Green said, "but it's still a hazard. The lights flash like there's a fire somewhere and then black out and it makes the audience panic. And that rancid smell of stale smoke! No one wants to spend time in the place. There was a time I thought I could rent it out for banquets and weddings. But there is also the matter of the ghost. A nasty despicable one too. It's been well-documented by a team of ghosthunters and that's been a death-knell for any future use of the place."

"My dear lady," answered the accountant, "times have changed. People want to go out at night again and live theater is a thrilling distraction. The Candlelight Theater is in the perfect location. I know I can keep a budget on track and hopefully an audience entertained. And if the shows don't offer an appropriate return on investment, maybe the ghost and its reputation might lure customers in as a bonus attraction."

"It's a spiteful tale," she said. "Remember that I warned you."

"I'm hoping to learn the backstory of the ghost," Mr. Meloso said. "And exploit it as much as I can."

A few weeks after this, the purchase was concluded and, at the close of Mr. Meloso's clients' tax season, the accountant and his partner took possession of the theater. Mr. Meloso's partner, Flynn Winters, had been a celebrated high school drama teacher in Candler, and was a handsome, middle-aged man, with fine eyes and a superb profile. Many handsome men upon discovering that they are handsome embark on a career in front of the camera or beneath the stage lights, under the impression that their God-given handsomeness is an expression of talent, but Mr. Winters had never fallen into this falsehood. He had a magnificent temperament, a wonderful amount of intelligence, and he knew he was more suited at being a teacher than a performer and, as he saw this new opportunity as he was also entering his fifties, it felt like a logical career progression to go from directing high school theatrical productions to becoming a professional director of a community theater. Indeed, in many respects, he was the perfect choice to direct a cast of local actors. Candler had a reputation of educating and sending away many hometown performers to Broadway, Hollywood, and amusement park stages.

In fact, Messrs. Meloso and Winters had already assembled their professional team based on Mr. Winters's previous interactions with community artists. Wendy Summers was young and fashion-conscious and an inspired choice to oversee every aspect of the theater's Media Relations; petite and plus-size, she was an expert social influencer, positioned to make the Candler followers who did not find her obnoxious and self-involved abandon their cell phones to replicate

her personal adventures. Wendy was certain her New Approaches to Old Media by Focusing on Me would keep the theater trending with activity. Scott Sparks was also a risky choice to be the Production Manager; a dark-eyed, dark-haired, dreamy-looking dreamer with ambitious, pot-inspired inventions and a low-key enthusiasm, he understood the mechanics of the husbandry arts that eluded his employers. A slow, philosophical and eco-sustainable carpenter and tradesman, he had worked on a backyard deck for the Messrs. Meloso and Winters that had also doubled as an outdoor-at-home art salon, the completion of which had inspired the purchase of the theater. Mr. Meloso's two nieces, Emily and Amy, a pair of sisters with long legs and incredulous, oversized eyes, were hired to handle the box office and administrative affairs, while secretly swapping fashion and makeup tips and harboring their own desires of attaining stardom if and when the right parts became available and did not require more effort than choosing appropriate outfits.

* * *

It was a dark and stormy April morning when work began to reopen the theater. Wade Griggs, a sixtysomething local contractor and construction foreman, came recommended by Mrs. Carroway-Green because of his history of trying to solve the problems of the building and the auditorium. Balding and stoic and sporting a bushy gray moustache, Mr. Griggs calmly escorted the new owners and their staff around the darkened theater with flashlights, then located a switch to a grumbly generator and explained the renovation diagrams in the dimly lit space.

Mr. Winters caught the smell of something burning and brought it to the attention of the foreman. Emily and Amy both began to sneeze and to check their shoulder bags for tissues. Wendy Summers complained that there was not enough available light for selfies and Scott Sparks disappeared from the auditorium, wandering off with a flashlight to explore the dark and unknown corners of the building on his own.

"It's an after smell," Mr. Griggs explained. "It's seeped into the carpets and the seat cushions and the curtains. Mrs. Green went through a costly process of having the whole theater cleaned and the stench still lingers."

Mr. Winters paced a few steps, then said, "But it's not wood smoke. It's cigarette smoke. I know that smell distinctly. I've chased it down on many of my students."

"The lady who perished was a heavy smoker," Mr. Griggs said. "It's rumored that it was the cause of the fire."

"We can find a way to mask the smell," Mr. Meloso said. "Cover it up with another smell. Something fruity or floral."

At that moment the generator abruptly gave up and the theater went black.

Mr. Griggs flipped on his flashlight again and said, "That ghost is going to be a problem."

Mr. Meloso and his partner assured the foreman that they were not afraid of a ghost and, after an exasperated discussion about the renovation budget and the timeline for completion, the foreman cautiously walked into the lobby and called in an electrician for advice.

* * *

William Carroway, one of the early settlers of Candler, owned the greatest part of the village and had opened its first business, a tavern, then built a store opposite it and set up a post office. The Great Fire of 1869 burned building after building, but a new row of brick buildings soon rose from the ashes. In 1877, J. B. Carroway inherited the property where the Candlelight Theater now stands, at the west end of Main Street where a firebreak had been created by tearing down a home on the site. A new brick structure was erected that housed the Carroway Printing Company, but as the family wealth grew and shrank and changed, the printing company relocated and the structure became home to a shirt factory until it was abandoned during the Great War and rediscovered in the 1920s by a group of artists and writers seeking inspiration outside of their urban jungle. The first productions at the newly named Candlelight Theater were lectures and art exhibits and plays presented by actors reciting from scripts on a candlelit stage. During the Second World War, the Carroway family held community dances and fundraisers for the war effort, until the structure was gutted by fire, rumored to have been started by one of the Carroway boys and a couple of rowdy servicemen on leave. Its replacement this time was a mishmash of decisions and mistakes made by owner Roland Carroway and his wife Madeline, the stage shrinking as wings were added for cooking and dining and overnight accommodations, all of which brought about additional hazards to the property.

Messrs. Meloso and Winters had been classmates at Candler High, suspecting each other as secretly being gay, each fumbling through the coming out process during the early, uncertain years of AIDS. Time away from village taught each of them self-respect and gave them goals, but their visible life together in Candler had been a progression from roommates to significant others to husband and husband. Years of volunteering and advocating in the community slowly washed away fears and mistrust; now, they were as deeply rooted in the history of Candler as the Carroways themselves.

After more blackouts and exasperated discussions, a new power grid and circuit board were installed at the theater. Mr. Griggs suggested installing an air-filtering system. It had not been in the budget, though Mr. Meloso had been able to navigate surcharges and overtime labor by striking deals for tickets and tax returns. Scott Sparks had replaced the stage lights and installed state-of-the-art light and sound boards he had won through online auctions and recreated the "groovy" candlelight effects that Messrs. Meloso and Winters were determined to incorporate and highlight in the performances. Wendy Summers posted video clips on the Internet of her reactions to samples of new lighting and sound effects that were guaranteed to scare away any lingering resident spirit and which had a link to a crowdfunding account set up by Emily and Amy. "I am literally standing on a spiritual footprint," Wendy Summers proclaimed into her cell-phone camera, "where actors will soon recreate all the dramas I face in my life." After a week of no hits or contributions in the web-sphere, a hasty decision was made to abort the online fundraising plan in favor of Mr. Winters announcing auditions for the first production.

By the end of the first month, Scott Sparks was standing outside the theater offering hits

off a joint to anxious stage moms and warning hopeful auditioners of areas with a fresh coat of paint. Despite the work of a number and variety of different air filters and the distribution of face masks, the smell of wet paint was everywhere. Mr. Meloso was proudly watching from the wings as his partner coached potential cast members, when he was startled by another curious smell wafting from stage left. It smelled like cigarette smoke and seemed to be getting stronger though no smoke or mist or fire was visible. He wandered behind the stage curtains and stopped when he reached the hallway that led to the backstage dressing rooms. Right in front of him he saw an overweight middle-aged woman wearing a loose-fitting pink cloth robe over a slip. Her face was covered by what looked to be a white cream that highlighted the fleshy rings beneath her eyes. Her gray hair was stretched out from her head into Medusa-like threads, as if she had unraveled it from curlers. In one hand she held a burning cigarette dramatically between two fingers, her elbow positioned against her stomach by the cupped palm of her other hand. Her eyes were burning red coals. She appeared to be watching a young woman on stage attempting to sing a ballad and Mr. Meloso had mistaken her for an impatient stage mother.

"Madame," Mr. Meloso said, "there is no smoking inside the theater. I must ask you to extinguish that at once."

For a moment the Candlelight ghost stood motionless in indignation of both the audition and the request; then, dashing the cigarette violently to the floor, she fled down the hallway, groaning and shrieking and casting a rippling shadow. As she reached a dressing room door, Wendy Summers jumped in front of her with her out-thrust cell phone, trying to capture herself with the spirit on video. Instead, only Wendy's spidery eyelash and a mysterious, whispery gasp were recorded and the ghost vanished from the hall.

On reaching a small hidden room behind the abandoned dining wing, the ghost took refuge on a convertible couch covered by a stiff, knit-wool blanket. She was indignant. She had endured weeks of hammering and banging but for what? An ingenue who could not hold a tune? A tenor who did not know how to cross the stage? She knew the difference between art and entertainment, though she didn't want to resume her revenge on the talentless and uneducated. She knew talent needed nurturing in order to shine. But she had grown comfortable over the last few years, a forgotten legend, and had finally reached peace with it. She had spent too many years torturing ushers and beauty queens, blowing fuses and yanking out circuits, destroying cues and creating confusion, and now this? Alive, she had made audiences weep with her slapstick and demand encores for her dramatics. Dead, she had progressed from the mere foolery of stealing props to knowing when it was better to levitate them. But this, this was unbearable. *Community theater? Amateur theatrics posing as professionals?* It could be expected when she was a gifted, aging actress on a career downswing, but no ghost confined to regret in perpetuity should ever have to endure this. *Sure, sure,* she thought, *everyone has to start somewhere. Experience is education.* She knew she should cut the young and hopeful some slack. But she was old and fed up and dead. She wanted to be left alone with her misery and now she had to prove herself *again* to achieve it.

* * *

The next morning the ghost was part of everyone's conversation. The video clip Wendy Summers had posted on her social media account was trending with comments expressing incredulity, ire, ridicule, and profanity.

By the time Scott Sparks arrived at the theater, Emily and Amy were distraught at the number of phone calls arriving on the office phone landlines, cornering Mr. Meloso into making an investment in an automated answering and ticketing website because they were feeling overwhelmed and overworked. Mr. Winters got involved in the discussion because he felt any further financial investments on behalf of the owning partners should be directed toward the stage productions, which Scott Sparks felt was like a "cool idea, 'cause then we could do some really awesome stuff."

"Any extra money we find should be reserved for the ghost," Mr. Meloso argued. "It's unpredictable.

We need to start a savings account. Our insurance rates are certain to go up."

"But we must do something!" Mr. Winters pleaded. "We can't have it disrupting performances!"

"We could trap it," Scott said. "Lure it into what it thinks is a safe space, like a bottle of something, and cork it."

"That's a bit cruel, don't you think?" Mr. Meloso said. "How would you like to live inside a glass bottle?"

"Depends on what else is inside," Scott replied.

"That ghost has been very good to me," Wade Griggs told Scott Sparks a few hours later. Mr. Meloso had called him to repair a leak that had started in the lobby restrooms. "As long as there's a ghost there's a lot of repairs that need to be done."

"You've seen it?" Scott asked.

"I've seen what it does," Wade Griggs answered. "That's good enough for me."

By evening, Mr. Meloso had taped a follow-up statement for Wendy Summers to distribute on all social media accounts. "We have no wish to exorcise the ghost," he said. "She—we think the ghost is a she—is an integral part of the history of our theater and our village. We invite her to be our guest at every performance, just not as the performance itself. If she remains unhappy or becomes a hazard to the theater, we will explore alternative locations for the ghost and gladly assist with relocating it."

For the rest of the week, auditions went undisturbed; the only thing that elicited any attention was an occasional smell of smoke inside the theater, even though a designated smoking area had been established at the edge of the parking lot and Mr. Meloso had made a concerted effort to announce its whereabouts in all crowded and empty rooms of the building.

Rehearsals began the following week. The theater's first production, *The Candlelight Follies,* was the brainchild of Mr. Winters, assembled from his personal archive of original cast recordings, used scripts, and photocopied programs. The format was to showcase as much local talent as possible and keep an audience of family and friends entertained.

During her surveillances, the ghost conceded that the follies was a good idea, at least from an initial economic standpoint, but she felt the "talent" involved was arguable, though she was willing to remain silent and nonjudgmental on this point. After all, her career had been determined by the judgment of others, but acting onstage had never prepared her to handle life offstage. Where was Chekov when a check bounced?

And so she was content with creating only minor mischief, something that would get her to leave her room on a daily basis and make her laugh and keep herself entertained. She targeted the piano player first, upending his music and then sitting on the keys, then she found a way to tap-tap-tap and send the dancers off count. She spent a good deal of time following Wade Griggs because he was a familiar face to her, misplacing his tools and tapping him on the shoulder to make him annoyed. She found she could fog up Mr. Winters's glasses so that he could not see the stage. She misplaced the files in the box office and blew smoke at Emily and Amy to make them sneeze. And she made Scott Sparks reboot the fuse box after every performer left the stage.

But Wendy Summers misstepped when she was promoting her "dance diet" and a promotional leotard from the Candler Spin Club and referred to the upcoming production at the renovated theater as a "community burlesque" in one of her cell-phone videos. Burlesque was a dirty word to the ghost—no performer, even a talentless and bosom-less one with chop shop hair, should have to sink that low, teasing and stripping to get applause. The ghost meant to put a stop to this. Her humor disappeared. She held her indignation through the failed attempt of young high school girls attempting a synchronized cancan routine, but when a young man—still clearly in his teens—came onstage and performed a breathtaking aria, a display of unparalleled talent that moved her to panic and despair knowing he would be overlooked and wasted in a local production, she let out a shriek that instantly sent the theater dark and she swept through the house, extinguishing every cell-phone light that flipped on until she reached the mezzanine. She shrieked again, this time as a warning meant for the production to cease, but the theater lights came back on and she was worried that she would be detected disheveled in her house-robe attire. Embarrassed, she retreated down a staircase as the cast and crew assessed this major interruption.

The ghost was chain-smoking when Mr. Meloso located her in the backstage hallway. "Madame," he began. "I don't know what is bothering you, but I must ask that you give up that nasty habit while you are inside the theater."

Her eyes went coal red. She was ready to release her full fury when she noticed Wendy Summers was nearby and recording the accountant with her cell phone. Upset and humiliated, she vanished through a wall, leaving in her wake a bizarre sound effect of angry guitar strums, or so Mr. Meloso thought.

* * *

The subject of the ghost arose when Mr. Meloso lunched with Sybil Carroway-Green at the Candler Tavern. It was intended as a friendly follow-up meeting after the purchase, though Mr. Meloso had a list of fundraising ideas he had hoped to present to the former owner to solicit her possible personal involvement. While her years of managing the Candlelight Theater had drained her of her family inheritance, her husband, the village dermatologist, had continued to subsidize her participation in the village's cultural activities, becoming a patron and sponsor of the community symphony and the annual art fair. Mr. Meloso's suggestions included founding a Garden Committee to help with the exterior grounds and floral displays inside the theater, an Artists Committee to oversee rotating art exhibitions in the lobby, and a Ladies Club to arrange for group sales to matinee performances. Mrs. Carroway-Green seemed disinterested in all these ideas, until Mr. Meloso raised the suggestion of adding a historical plaque to the theater. "We might be able to get landmark status," he said, "though that process is long and involves all sorts of paperwork. I was thinking of something more immediate and press worthy. Of course, we would mention your father."

Matthew Carroway had been a hometown success story. In fact, he was Candler's biggest national story, or, perhaps, most famous local legend. A high school and college track and field athlete, he served in the Pacific fleet and became a national hero for pushing a raft of injured sailors to safety. After returning from World War II, he landed stage roles in New York until he caught the great television wave and moved to Hollywood. His success with staring in and producing the newly developed sitcom television format made him wealthy and a notorious womanizer. His first and second marriages crumbled because of his indiscretions. After his second ex-wife's death in a suspicious car accident, his eight-year-old daughter Sybil came to live with her grandparents in Candler. Matthew Carroway was in his fifties when he inherited the Candlelight Theater after his father's death, though he left the day-to-day running of the theater to his mother, his first ex-wife, and later his daughter. Though his return to Candler had been promoted as a triumphant homecoming, he was resentful about leaving the national limelight behind and had no tolerance for a teenage daughter, except when it came to entertaining her girlfriends.

"My father was a complicated man," Mrs. Carroway-Green said. "I'm grateful that his career and personal life have been remained overlooked and unexamined. I'd like to keep it that way."

"I saw your father perform several times at the Candlelight when I was a boy," Mr. Meloso said. "My parents took me and my sister as much as they could afford. He was such a gifted actor. He and Shirley Arden were mesmerizing on stage together."

Shirley Arden had been Matthew Carroway's first wife. They had costarred as a couple for four seasons in a popular television sitcom before the scandal of Matthew Carroway's sexual relationship with an underaged girl caused the network executives to cancel the show. The couple divorced shortly thereafter, and even though their Hollywood careers suffered, they continued their professional relationship in a succession of stage tours. When Matthew became the owner of the Candlelight Theater, he hired Shirley as a costar for a repertory season. She was such a success—or a relief, depending on sources—Matthew hired her to manage the theater, and after his death, she continued until a succession of fires halted everything.

"They hated each other till the very end," Mrs. Carroway-Green said. "That's probably why she still haunts the theater."

Surprised, Mr. Meloso responded, "The ghost is Shirley Arden? I thought that was a rumor."

"Mrs. Arden was as complicated as my father," she said. "At times she was like a second mother to me, but she would never let me succeed with that theater because it had always been a battle for her. She was *bitter.* A very, very bitter woman."

* * *

In her hidden room behind the dining hall, the ghost began to question her purpose. It was one thing to impede Sybil Carroway-Green and continue to ruin the Carroway family name in any manner she could devise, but now that the family was no longer associated with the Candlelight it was never her intention to destroy a theater and set about to ruin talent. The theater had always been like a home to her. It gave her confidence and a purpose. To perform in front of an audience was her antidote for loneliness.

When she was a teenager, her family had moved out of the city and she had discovered summer stock, working in the box office and backstage so she could have a walk-on role to move a prop. In those first years, she never felt alone in the theater. The theater made her feel special but also smartened her up—gave her a style and an education and a point of view. She loved the theater so much she dropped out of high school and moved to Manhattan and became a Broadway success. Not at first, of course. Her notices toughened her up and made her better. She was panned as a "mumbler," a "bug-eyed psycho" and a "bewildered scrap of broccoli." She failed completely as Viola, Saint Joan, and Hedda, but it gave her the ability to laugh at herself. A comedy role in a popular radio series caught the attention of Hollywood producers and she journeyed across country to Los Angeles where she met Matthew Carroway. She was great at comedy and that made her even better with drama. Even those early years in Hollywood seemed idyllic now, compared to the obstacles that had forced her to relocate to Candler.

For days she hardly stirred out of her room, except to blow smoke through the ventilation shafts, but she felt isolated, never a good thing for a person who seeks response and applause. She floated into the theater and watched Scott Sparks run through the stage candlelight effects, flickering lights at the lip of the stage. This made her happy; she had created this trademark effect at the beginning and end of every performance at the theater; one year, she had even hired a lighting designer noted for his nightclub effects to have the flickering lights dance in time to the musical overture. It pleased her now to see that the renovated theater would be continuing the tradition.

She placed a hand against the young man's heart—as a ghost she had a gift she seldom used, the ability to see a person's dreams. *A musician? A band?* So Scott wanted to start his own band? As she imagined the music he might create she was consumed by her own memories. She withdrew her hand, as if it had been burned. Scott stopped his working and caught the notes of a song playing somewhere in the theater. He listened. It was guitar music, with intricate finger work and a plucked melody. He reached into his back pocket for a small notebook and pencil and jotted down a phrase. *A songwriter?* the ghost thought, and then she floated away.

The ghost drifted through the backstage area. There were girls getting dressed, practicing their lines and routines, dressers patching costumes, the stage manager was setting up props. She was fascinated and intrigued, making a young girl lose her concentration and recite her lines over and over. At some point she realized that tonight was the first public performance for the reopened theater. She thought about doing some misdeed, but as she felt it important to break her old habits, she was fighting to remain out of mischief. Her antagonists were the Carroways, not these wannabe, some good some not-so-good actors. This was the theater, the palace of dreams.

She floated up to the mezzanine, flickering lights to spot check her powers. If only she could have had this power while alive. A magic beyond imagination. She could cause distress by blowing wind or making an eerie sound. If only she could have done this while young and alive—she would have made those critics eat their words.

The theater was beginning to fill up with patrons. She took the staircase to the lobby and watched the young girls in the box office. She knew they were phonies, but each one was impressionable. Time and tears and setbacks would give them truths. At some point she noticed the lobby had been decorated with photographs. She drifted closer to inspect them. Her disbelief came first. They were photos of Matthew Carroway, his father, his mother, and his daughter and her husband. She went from photo to photo, reading the captions that glorified the Carroway family and their support of the theater. A project curated by Sybil Carroway-Green. Praise after praise after praise. And not a photo or mention of Shirley Arden and her dedication and devotion in sight.

The ghost made the wind move first, just as a warning breeze, then as a roaring gale. Guests in the lobby scattered to move out of a growing funnel of air, hands lifted to protect their eyes. She sent the photos crashing to the floor, amplifying the sound of shattering glass.

How dare they glorify this family of liars and thieves and criminals! She hated this family, hated her links and ties and servitude to them.

She blew through the auditorium doors, flopping down seat cushions with a booming force—boom, boom, boom, boom, BOOM. She flew up to the antique chandelier and thought about ripping it out of the ceiling and sending it crashing to the floor, but instead flew into the wiring and sent the theater dark. In the blackout, her scream pierced through the auditorium and backstage darkness. Fear rattled through the building. Nervous sounds flew about like startled birds.

Mr. Winters was in the wings when the power went out. He gasped and let out an anguished sigh. He waited a second, hoping the power would be restored, and then touched his cell-phone light app and began to tell the cast and crew not to panic. "Stay calm, everyone," he said.

In the lobby, Mr. Meloso was urging his customers to remain calm, saying that it was all "part of the experience of attending the Candlelight Theater." He used a flashlight to illuminate his face. The ushers flipped on their handheld flashlights, checking tickets and leading people to their seats. A general sense of laughter and adventure began to displace the anxiety and uneasiness. Tiny flashlights began to click on. Mr. Meloso had prepared for this likelihood, investing in complimentary small lights that had been distributed as ticketholders entered the lobby.

Offstage, Scott Sparks reached the new solar-powered generator and flipped the switch, restoring small rows of dim lights throughout the building. Wade Griggs had declared the system ghost-proof, and it sent a calming effect throughout the building.

Mr. Meloso climbed the steps and stopped centerstage. "Welcome, welcome!" he addressed the audience. "The Candlelight Theater is proud to reopen tonight with our first performance in thirteen years and to welcome back to the theater our resident ghost. Rumor has it that she may be in attendance at every performance, and we are so glad she is here with us tonight. What a special treat! As you see she has already started her mischief but never fear, the show will go on! Our actors and crew have prepared to entertain you even in the event of a blackout." Next, Mr. Meloso waved his hands theatrically and said, "Voilà!" and a row of battery-operated candle lights illuminated the stage floor of the theater.

The audience applauded. The response was so loud and joyous the sound reached the ghost in her hidden room behind the dining hall. She knew she should be thankful that no one was harmed with her mischief, but her fury was overwhelming her. She had been outwitted. She had been turned into a sideshow. A joke. Now she was humiliated and angry.

* * *

The Candlelight Follies was a hometown success, but as the ghost's disruptions escalated, battle lines were drawn. There were discussions between Messrs. Meloso and Winters on whether the Candlelight ghost was real and then whether a bogus ghost could become a bogus lawsuit with real, monetary punitive damages. At the heart of the conversations were the potential consequences, but most importantly what the future might bring.

What if someone were hurt and sued? What if they had to sell the theater?

"We could lose everything," Mr. Winters said.

"It's not about the money," Mr. Meloso replied. "We could always get real jobs."

"Real jobs?" Mr. Winters answered. "What do you think this is? Do you know how hard I've worked to get here?"

"We've both worked hard for this," Mr. Meloso said. "This is a dream, Flynn. We both wanted to do this so much. Neither of us want it to become a nightmare. There is always something else we could do."

"Don't you understand, Otto? There is nothing else but the theater. I'm not giving up."

In an effort to resolve their own dramatics, the partners drove to the village library and watched a video tape of the ghosthunting episode that was filmed at the theater years before, but the investigation was an exercise in bad theatrics by dull, overweight men who badly needed haircuts and shaves and probably showers, relying on gasps and fuzzy camera glass smears and jerking handheld technology that did not seem to function, only to end with the open question that began the episode—who was the ghost at the Candlelight Theater? Was it the unlucky actress Shirley Arden, a drunk serviceman on leave, or a disgruntled actor from the 1920s? Or could it even be hometown favorite Matthew Carroway?

Mr. Winters felt the ghosthunters might have benefitted from some professional acting classes and coaching sessions. "Were you even scared?" he asked Mr. Meloso. "Were you even entertained?"

Nonetheless, this exploration into ghosthunting led to another discussion between the men: What if wasn't a ghost at all?

"What if someone is targeting us?" Mr. Winters worried.

"Like a crime?"

"Yes, because..."

"Because...we're in the theater?" Mr. Meloso said. He grew concerned, then troubled. "We've never had that problem before. I know it could be an issue, but I'd rather think that it was a ghost."

"Could the ghost be...you know, anti-...um, homophobic?"

"It's a theater, how could it be?"

"But that could be why it's so annoyed with us."

"I don't think it is targeting us," Mr. Meloso decided. "Sybil Carroway warned us. It was disclosed in the deed. She thinks it's Shirley Arden because there was some kind of bad blood between her father and Shirley. But whatever is happening, it needs to stop. If it is a ghost, we need to get rid of it. Even if it *is* Shirley Arden."

This caused Mr. Winters a great deal of concern. "You can't distinguish it," Mr. Winters said. "It's a ghost. A lost spirit. Of someone who was once here. A real person. On earth. It's searching for some answer or resolution. We need to help it."

"Now you want us to help a ghost that may or may not be homophobic?" Mr. Meloso replied. "Did you see the repair bill Wade Griggs left? We need to get rid of it. Maybe we should hire an exorcist."

"You can't exorcise a demon that hasn't possessed someone," Mr. Winters replied. "No one's been possessed. We need to help it find peace."

"You're wrong," Mr. Meloso said. "Someone has been possessed. *You!* You've turned stark raving mad."

And then the partners drew battle lines that each was hesitant to cross—Mr. Winters handled the backstage mishaps; Mr. Meloso took the front-of-the-house headaches. Only the stage seemed to coexist peacefully between the men, mostly because the ghost felt no urge to be judgmental to a performer. Instead, costumes were ripped into shreds and makeup melted or was pounded into dust. The framed photographs in the lobby were rehung in unbreakable plexiglass mounts, but they were ripped from the wall and tossed to the floor. The walls suffered damages, as if a malevolent child had socked them with a superhuman fist.

It was Wade Griggs who led the new owners to their next course of action. While helping a contractor install a new windowpane because the ghost—or some other unknown unnatural force—had shattered it, he mentioned that Sybil Carroway-Green had once used a spiritualist to cleanse the building and it had produced a soothing effect, at least for a short period of time.

Françoise Demanier, who still lived in a neighboring town, arrived on a damp, gray, misty morning to shake holy water and rattle a burning

sage bouquet about the property. By now she was in her midnineties and held upright with the help of a cane and the arm of Wade Griggs. Wendy Summers captured the return visit on her cell phone, posing the first question to the spiritualist: "Do you think I should add sage to my diet?"

Françoise's hearing was compromised by the sound of her necklaces and bracelets that rattled as she moved. She was swathed in an oversized magenta caftan that was pinned the height of a cocktail skirt, revealing a pair of thin-strapped pink stiletto heels at the end of her tiny legs. "Sage won't help the ego," she replied into Wendy's cell phone.

It was a slow, dramatic process to lead Françoise around the property. "I'd love to have another chat with Shirley," she told Mr. Meloso as she waved a bouquet of smoking sage in the lobby. "She cast me in a few productions, you know. But I had such problems remembering all the lines. She was a consummate professional. She told me to understand the character and the situation and then say what I felt. She got me through some rough spots onstage and off. She never got the credit she deserved for keeping this theater running. It was love, you know. She loved that boy. That boy was everything to her. She was always so thankful for Wade."

Messrs. Meloso and Winters glanced at Wade Griggs, expecting him to add a response. He stood tall and remained quiet and introspective, deflecting the attention turned toward him by gazing down at Françoise. Wade Griggs never had much to say unless it had to do with a repair and, at that moment, both partners grew suspicious of him, aware they knew little personal details about their overpriced foreman who provided the theater with handyman services, someone to whom they had been handing over large sums of money on a regular basis. But both men knew that they could not demand answers: Who are your people? Who do you vote for? What, in fact, do you think of theater folk?

Instead, Mr. Meloso tried another tact. "I suppose we keep forgetting how long you've been helping the theater," he said. "You used to work for Shirley Arden, right?

"She gave me my first job," Wade Griggs answered.

"Do you think the ghost is Shirley Arden?" Mr. Meloso asked.

"That would mean admitting that I believe in ghosts," Wade Griggs answered.

"Is she a good ghost or a bad ghost?" Mr. Winters asked. "If she is a ghost."

The ghost hovered close by, watching and listening and blowing the smoke from Françoise Demanier's sage bouquet until it forced Wendy Summers to stop recording herself. As the partners grew suspicious of Wade Griggs, the ghost protectively encircled him.

"It's complicated for sure," Wade Griggs answered. "I don't think Shirley Arden would want to be any kind of ghost at all, unless there was a demand for her to do it onstage, in front of an audience."

"So you believe she's the ghost?" Mr. Meloso asked.

Wade Griggs hesitated, but Françoise Demanier provided an answer. "Oh, of course, it's Shirley Arden. She's here right now, by the way. I can feel her energy. Sybil never wanted to admit it and never

wanted to talk to her. But we could summon her to speak with us. I'm sure she has lots to tell."

Mr. Meloso was reluctant to schedule a formal séance, worried more about time and expenses and logistics than the outcome, but Mr. Winters was all for an on-the-spot impromptu summoning. "Can you speak with her now?" he asked Françoise. "We'd love to see her happy again. Is there somewhere else she would rather be? Maybe we could move her to another location?"

The impromptu séance was just that. Scott Sparks was located and asked to lower the house lights and Françoise Demanier was positioned in a theater seat near the lip of the stage. She closed her eyes to meditate and promptly fell asleep. After a minute, Wendy Summers whispered to Mr. Meloso that the spiritualist must be a fake, loud enough, of course, to be picked up by her cell-phone microphone to make Internet postings possible, but not loud enough to wake Françoise .

In the quiet moments that followed, however, the ghost stayed close to Wade Griggs who stayed close to Françoise. The ghost thought about how the once-young man had aged nicely. The creased lines at his eyes, the crevices of his cheeks, the shiny bald scalp ringed with gray-white hairs. She had been reluctant to know how deeply he missed his past, but now, sitting quietly together as if they were old friends, she placed her hand against his chest.

The sorrow was immediate and deep, but she kept her hand in place, knowing there was nothing she could do to repair this.

A few minutes later, when Françoise stirred, she looked up at Wade Griggs and said, "I know you, don't I?" It was enough to convince everyone she was too old and fragile and potentially senile to facilitate a séance. When Françoise realized where she was, she asked Wade Griggs to drive her back to her home. "It takes so much out of me," she said. "Theater folk are so self-absorbed."

As she was leaving, she thanked Mr. Meloso and handed him an invoice and a gift basket of sage and violet oils. "I can come back if you need me," she said. "Shirley isn't your only problem."

* * *

A suspicious peace followed; there was a shared belief that Françoise Demanier's visit had been successful at eradicating the presence of the ghost of Shirley Arden. The myth was perpetuated first by Mr. Meloso talking candidly with Wendy Summers while she filmed their conversation and was later echoed by Mr. Winters in an announcement to the cast before an evening performance. In private, the co-owners had decided to adopt an "out of sight, out of mind" strategy in regards to the Candlelight ghost in hopes that she would not make encore performances. "The best reaction is not to react," Mr. Meloso now said to his partner. "We have to believe that there is no such thing as a ghost."

But skepticism remained. Emily and Amy, unnerved by a sequence of heavy breathing telephone callers on the box office phone lines, blamed the ghost for the static and creepy noises, though Scott Sparks determined the cause was faulty wireless earplugs. Wendy Summers blamed the ghost when her cell phone failed to record and powered off during a heavy rainstorm; she had witnessed a sudden banging of doors, a blast of cold air, and felt a mist of water settling onto the vintage outfit she was modeling courtesy of the Candler Antique Market. Scott Sparks was perplexed by a sequence of flashing lights on his sound effects board monitor and, using a Morse code translator he downloaded from the Internet, determined the sequence spelled out, "Fire in the hole," though later, when he discussed it with Wade Griggs, they modified the probable message from the ghost to mean, "Don't forget to water the plants."

It was less than a week later when Mr. Winters was rehearsing on stage and found it impossible to concentrate or communicate with his performers. Because of the success of *The Candlelight Follies,* new acts were needed as cast members required time off for personal matters and the co-owners had made an arrangement of free tickets with the community Office for the Aging for acts sponsored by the Candler Seniors Club. Mr. Winters's rehearsal had been plagued by a series of interruptions—flashing lights, microphone issues, and a general lack of ability of a group of senior citizens to learn choreography. The sound of other rehearsals in the building was bleeding through the wings and onto the stage. Music would start and stop, long enough for Mr. Winters and the elderly performers to forget its intrusion, and then it would return, loud guitar strums and intricate melody lines. Exasperation made the director call for a break and he took the opportunity to follow the sound of music through the backstage rooms.

The sound was strongest from a corridor outside the abandoned dining hall. Mr. Winters paused to listen, an attempt to also take a breath, relax, and minimize his frustration. It was beautiful music, a guitar line so ethereal and mesmerizing it could be mistaken for a harp. As he stood quietly in the corridor listening, Mr. Winters could also sense a gathering presence around him. "Please stop," he whispered politely. "Miss Arden, this must stop."

The music stopped and the silence that followed felt both blissful and dangerous, like a tidal wave was creeping toward the shore.

The scream flattened Mr. Winters, a sound of pain so shattering he stumbled and fell. "In all my years of directing, I've never heard anything like this," he would later tell Mr. Meloso. "It was awful. Anger laced with anguish."

* * *

A few days later, Scott Sparks decided to check the wiring in the abandoned dining hall. Wade Griggs had mentioned it was where a fire had originated years before and the wing had been sealed off; Messrs. Meloso and Winters had said the renovation of it was now on hold, depending on a new budget. Scott unlocked the door and flipped the light switch but there was no light. He was about to leave to check the fuse box when he heard a startled gasp.

In the distant part of the room, he could see a woman seated at a table, barely visible because of the light that spilled through the window behind her. A faint sound of music—an acoustic guitar—could be heard playing a tune.

"I didn't mean to scare you," Scott said. He thought she was one of the elderly performers and stepped closer to the table to mention that the room was a dangerous place to rehearse, when he saw that it was the ghost. The Candlelight Ghost. She was dressed in a robe. Her hair spread out from her head in smoking, snake-like wings. Her posture seemed to indicate she was depressed. Or annoyed. A cigarette was burning in her hand.

"You didn't startle me," she said. "You reminded me of someone."

As they regarded each other the music became louder and then abruptly stopped in a disturbing way. Scott knew this opportunity might not happen again. He was searching for the right question to ask, when the ghost said, "I'm not about to leave this place. The more you try, the worse it's going to get."

"Mr. Meloso likes having you here," he said. "It's been good for business. Mr. Winters is more skeptical, but he does like the way every performance adapts to your presence."

She seemed to smile, flattered. "Spontaneity keeps the theater alive."

"The mischief is fine," he said. "They're concerned that it could...create a liability. Someone could get hurt."

"Someone did get hurt," she said.

"What happened?" Scott asked.

Her face registered a life of decisions. "What if?" she answered. "What if Matthew Carroway had never heard me on the radio? What if he had never ruined my career? What if his family had never owned this firetrap?"

"What caused the fire?" Scott asked. "Can we prevent it from happening again?"

"The fire was an accident," she said. "But it was the result of a sequence of events. I made decisions. For years, I made decisions. I accept the decisions I made. But the blame belongs to the Carroways."

She rose from her seat and approached Scott. "And how peaceful is your heart?"

The ghost spread into a looming presence, hovering before Scott, her arms stretching higher into a mist of smoke. It was an unsettling effect. Scott's instinct was to walk away, practice his breathing to maintain his composure, but some greater force kept him bolted into place.

"Your sister died when she was, what…three?" the ghost said. "Your mother could not bear the grief. Your father, where is he…now? That's right, you don't know. You don't care because he left you behind. So you're the one who's scared now. Scared of love. Of finding it. Of fighting for it. Of losing it…."

The anguish of his past anchored Scott's mind; sorrow, regret, unhappiness, and grief ran through his body and settled into his eyes.

"Self-medication will only grant you limited insight," the ghost said. "Follow me."

Scott hesitated because his feet still felt weighted to the ground. Then, the ghost walked through him. It was like a stinging, arctic wind had suddenly pierced him. The ghost turned and said, "Trust me and I will explain."

He saw the ghost pass through a wall, then realized he was no longer in the dining room. He was in a room that no longer existed, a room that had been destroyed by a fire. As he moved deeper into the room, items began to have focus and weight. The room was a home. There was a table and chairs. A stove. A refrigerator. A small table with a television. Against the wall was a bed. And there was someone in it.

* * *

That evening when the stage manager announced the half-hour call, Scott did not appear to run the light and sound boards. As Scott was in the habit of roaming through the building, inspecting and writing down what repairs were needed, Mr. Winters was not at all alarmed at first, but when the ten-minute notice was announced and Scott did not appear, he became agitated, and sent Wendy Summers to look for him, while he and Mr. Meloso searched every room in the theater. The stage manager filled in at the light board and Mr. Winters took over as the stage manager and the performance went on with only a few glitches. But Scott's truck was still in the theater parking lot and this caused the co-owners great concern.

After the performance, there was a second late-night hunt through the building and then another. Scott was nowhere to be found. His cell phone was still active but could not be heard ringing in any part of the building and there had been no response from the repeated voice and text messages sent to him.

In private, Messrs. Meloso and Winters had a discussion about whether to contact the village police and then, in front of the remaining staff, announced that Scott had been reached and was at

his apartment. It was a great feat of acting on the part of Mr. Winters to portray himself as calm and relieved when he was just the opposite. After the building had been vacated and everyone was safely on their way home, Messrs. Meloso and Winters waited in the small office behind the box office window.

It was evident that something had happened to Scott. Mr. Winters was out of his mind with terror and anxiety, blaming himself and dealing with the aftershock of his hiding the truth of this from others. Mr. Meloso tried to piece together any forgotten clues. Scott was not a minor; he was not dating anyone. He lived alone. He was not being stalked. His pot was dispensed from a legal shop. His life revolved around the Candlelight Theater. If he wasn't working at the theater, he was in his truck running errands for the theater. The only oddity was a guitar that had been seen behind the front seat of Scott's truck.

"It's always been there," Mr. Meloso said. "I think it was there when he bought that truck."

"But Scott doesn't play guitar, does he?" Mr. Winters asked. "I've never seen him with a guitar."

Neither of the co-owners was willing to call the police. And neither gentleman was willing to leave the theater and attempt to sleep and wait at their house for further news. Both men ran through possible scenarios, aloud and to themselves.

"He's had some kind of accident," Mr. Winters said. "He fell somewhere we can't find him."

"We've checked everywhere," Mr. Meloso said. "We can't put a bell around his neck and monitor his every move."

"There must be a sealed-up well somewhere," Mr. Winters added. "Or a hidden dumbwaiter."

"There's nothing like that here."

"How do you know? How well did we know this place when we bought it? How well do we know this place now? There is always something turning up. I bet the ghost has something to do with this. I must have angered her. This is all my fault."

"We agreed that there was no ghost," Mr. Meloso said "so we don't drive ourselves crazy."

"But we are driving ourselves crazy looking for some kind of explanation for what is happening. And now it's happened to Scott. Scott's a part of this theater. He's an employee. That means he's family. While he's here we're responsible for him," Mr. Winters said. "Don't you get that?"

"I do," Mr. Meloso said softly.

The two men fell into a worrisome silence, aware that they perhaps did not know a "member of the family" as well as they thought they did. At some point they adjusted themselves in the uncomfortable office chairs and agreed that a new search through the building in the morning might turn up a clue, and, if not, they would contact the police. Then, they sat and stewed and thought and worried until they could close their eyes for a few minutes of restless sleep.

But the empty building remained frightening. The partners were conscious of every sound: the movement of the wind, the expansion of the floorboards, the deafening tick of the second hand of the lobby wall clock. Sometime, close to four o'clock in the morning, a dreadful peal of thunder shook the theater, awakening the co-owners. They ran through the lobby and into the theater, across the stage and into the backstage dressing rooms. They finally found Scott, looking pale and tired, in the abandoned dining hall.

"I've been with the ghosts," Scott said quietly.

"Ghosts?" Mr. Meloso asked. "There's more than one?"

* * *

Four days later, Mr. Meloso recorded a video announcing the theater would be renamed "The Shirley Arden Candlelight Theater."

"The Candlelight Theater is proud of its tradition and history and our survival and success is due to the innovative talents of the award-winning actress Shirley Arden, who managed and performed and directed at the theater for many years. She was the heart and soul of a successful community theater. Miss Arden and her son, Jody Arden, both perished in a fire that destroyed a portion of the theater buildings. There has always been a rumor that Shirley Arden was the Candlelight Ghost, and if that is so, then we are proud and pleased that the Candlelight Ghost will have a permanent home at the theater."

A public celebration for the renaming was planned for later that month, just as the theater's summer stock season was beginning to unfold. An historical plaque commemorating the lives of the Ardens—both Shirley and Jody—and their dedication to the theater would be installed in the theater's lobby. Mr. Meloso did not take any phone calls from Sybil Carroway-Green or answer any of her emails and texts and, when she appeared one morning at the theater to protest the new plans, he asked her to leave at once. "I can publicly shame the Carroway family by recirculating old news," he told her. "Or I can bring to light new stories. But I think both of us would like to avoid any attorney fees."

The new story was a complicated and forgotten one, pieced together again by Scott Sparks, the co-owners, and the village librarian. Down on her luck and not able to get any stage work in New York, Shirley Arden had moved to Candler and leased the theater from the Carroways, specifically her ex-husband, and to save on expenses she lived in a room behind the dining hall with her teenaged son. Joseph "Jody" Arden was fourteen when he transferred to Candler High. His classmate was Wade Griggs. As teenagers, Jody and Wade did odd jobs and handyman repairs for the theater, even performing cameos and walk-on performances when the task was required. Shirley Arden ran the Candlelight Theater for seventeen years, using a scheme of invoicing the Carroway family for fake repair bills for the theater to finance sending her son to college and beginning his career in New York.

Jody Arden's passion was music, not theater. He had begun teaching himself music at the age of five and after college, he played cover versions on his guitar in Washington Square Park until he joined a band that began playing his original "ethereal folk-rock" compositions. As the band landed more late-night gigs, Jody's youthful experimentation with drugs became an addiction.

At thirty-four and in the last stages of AIDS, unable to pay his bills and rent in New York, Jody was brought back to Candler to live with his mother at the theater. Wade Griggs was a daily visitor, monitoring IV bags and picking up medications. Jody Arden continued to compose new songs on his guitar up to his death. Jody was the son of Shirley and Matthew Carroway, conceived and born in the year before they were married and the popular sitcom began to air. Shirley's out-of-wedlock baby was kept out of the news and Matthew would never acknowledge paternity. As Jody had grown up and publicly come out as gay, any acknowledgment or reconciliation with the Carroway family had seemed more unlikely. Shirley blamed the Carroway cold shoulder for much of Jody's problems, though she admitted she might have initiated some of it herself by not telling him of his father until he was on his own career path in New York. Sybil Carroway, eight years younger than Jody, had also been kept in the dark, unaware that Jody was her half-brother until his final return to Candler.

In Shirley's opinion, Jody should have inherited the Carroway wealth, including the Candlelight Theater, though she never let her bitterness affect her relationship with her son or her performances onstage. But regret haunted Shirley when she was alive. And dead, Shirley was never at rest as long as the Carroways continued to own the theater. As a resident tenant, either alive or dead, she made it her goal to force her landlords to do any and every repair possible or impossible to the point of financial ruin. If Sybil Carroway had not sold the theater to Messrs. Meloso and Winters, foreclosure and bankruptcy was imminent, largely, it is believed, due the damages inflicted by the ghost. Mr. Meloso, as tax consultant to the town of Candler, was aware of the Carroway family's financial issues.

In the newspaper account of a backroom fire at the Candlelight Theater that claimed the life of Shirley Arden, the village fire chief noted that the fire possibly began when an electric space heater overturned and set aflame the pages of a playscript. Shirley succumbed to smoke inhalation. A burning cigarette was not involved, but it became the stuff of legend, as obituaries featured a photograph of Shirley Arden smoking at a rehearsal. Sybil Carroway-Green, as the owner of the theater, had the details of Jody's illness withheld from publication and she refused to admit that Jody was her half-brother. In news reports and on his death certificate, Jody Arden's cause of death was by "accident," and his life and music were overlooked and forgotten.

Months later, when Sybil Carroway-Green had Wade Griggs repair the dining hall, the small room behind the kitchen was not rebuilt. It was demolished and the dining hall was sealed up with a new brick wall, as if the room had never existed. According to Scott Sparks, Shirley's need for revenge stemmed from the family's inability to recognize her son in life or death, but the ghost of Shirley Arden would never be at peace until the spirit of Jody Arden was recognized and commended.

When Wade Griggs was next at the Candlelight, Mr. Meloso pulled him aside and asked him if he would be willing to do a specific job for him and his partner. Messrs. Meloso and Winters wanted to relocate the graves of Shirley Arden and her son at the Candler cemetery so that they were side by side and to give them better memorials. "I've checked with the cemetery management and the village officials and it's permissible. Though I need the sign off of the holder of the existing plots."

Wade Griggs stood quietly in front of Mr. Meloso. "I know you can't imagine that I was ever young," he said. "But Jody was my first...friend. We met in high school. He broke my heart and then came back and did it again."

Wade Griggs continued his tale. “Sybil would not pay for the burials. She was young and worried about the scandal of the fire and the rising costs of running the theater and she was keeping a lot of details from her husband. They had just been married. I found a way to pay for the plots, but I couldn’t afford to put them side by side.”

“But you did the right thing,” Mr. Meloso said. “And the theater will now pay for the relocation and any expenses.”

“Miss Arden knew what Jody meant to me,” Wade Griggs said. “She hired me to help out at the theater. She was good to me. So I kept coming back to help her. I needed the work. Even when Sybil took over, I think Miss Arden was always looking out for me.”

As he was leaving, Mr. Meloso said to Wade Griggs. “You’ve always been a friend of this theater. Flynn and I are thinking about changes. We’d be honored if you would join our new board of directors. We want to do a tribute performance of Jody Arden’s music and thought you might want to be involved with planning it.”

It would be another year before the graves of Shirley Arden and her son Jody were placed side by side at the village cemetery and given new memorial headstones. The event was marked by a festival of performances sponsored by the theater. Sybil Carrington-Green was not invited. Scott Sparks was the headline performer. Emily and Amy sang a duet. Wade Griggs shared a dance with Françoise Demanier, who also provided a special incantation for the celebration. Wendy Summers modeled her most recent product endorsement and recorded the event with her cell phone. Messrs. Meloso and Winters toasted each other in public. And in this brief intermission, all went undisturbed from the secrets of the dead.

SHIRLEY ARDEN
CANDLELIGHT THEATER
WELCOME

Jameson Currier is the author of seven novels: *Where the Rainbow Ends, The Wolf at the Door, The Third Buddha, What Comes Around, The Forever Marathon, A Gathering Storm,* and *Based on a True Story*; five collections of short fiction: *Dancing on the Moon; Desire, Lust, Passion, Sex; Still Dancing: New and Selected Stories; The Haunted Heart and Other Tales*; and *Why Didn't Someone Warn You About Prince Charming?*; and a memoir, *Until My Heart Stops*. His most recent publications are his illustrated tales: *Paul's Cat, The Devil's Cake, The Candlelight Ghost,* and *Mr. Darcy's Pride*. His short fiction has appeared in many literary magazines and Web sites, including *Velvet Mafia, Confrontation, Christopher Street,* and the anthologies *Men on Men, Best American Gay Fiction, Best Gay Stories, Wilde Stories,* and *Making Literature Matter*. In 2005, his AIDS-themed short stories were translated into French by Anne-Laure Hubert and published as *Les Fantômes* and in 2021, his novel, *The Third Buddha,* about the aftermath of 9/11 in Manhattan and Afghanistan, was translated into French by Étienne Gomez and published as *Le Troisième Bouddha* by Perspective cavaliere and was awarded the Prix du Roman Gay. His reviews, essays, interviews, and articles on AIDS and gay culture have been published in many national and local publications, including *The Washington Post, The Los Angeles Times, Lambda Book Report, The Washington Blade, Bay Area Reporter, The New York Blade, Out,* and *Body Positive.* In 2010 he founded Chelsea Station Editions, an independent press devoted to gay literature. Among the authors the press has published are debut writers Alan Lessik, Jarret Neal, J.L. Weinberg, Gil Cole, J.R. Greenwell, David Pratt, and William Sterling Walker, and veterans Kevin Bentley, Arch Brown, and Jon Marans. The press also serves as the home for Mr. Currier's own writings which now span a career of more than four decades. Books published by the press have been honored by the Lambda Literary Foundation, the American Library Association GLBTRT Roundtable, the Saints and Sinners Literary Festival, the Gaylactic Spectrum Awards Foundation, the Publishing Triangle, and the Rainbow Book Awards. In 2011, Mr. Currier launched the literary magazine *Chelsea Station,* which has published the works of more than two hundred writers and in 2014 relaunched the magazine as an online literary site. A self-taught artist, illustrator, and graphic designer, Mr. Currier's design work is tagged as "Peachboy" and his original art is signed "Jimmy." In 2020, he established Chatham Junction Studio, which serves as the curator for his expanding body of original art. Mr. Currier has been a member of the Board of Directors of the Arch and Bruce Brown Foundation, a recipient of a fellowship from New York Foundation for the Arts, and a judge for many literary competitions. He currently divides his time between a studio apartment in New York City and a farmless farmhouse in the Hudson Valley.

CPSIA information can be obtained
at www.ICGtesting.com
Printed in the USA
BVHW020349160223
658635BV00005B/106